I am Quetzal

BY ADDER A. ARGUETA

ILLUSTRATED BY ANA RODIC

Chapter 1 Home Sweet Home

There was a loud rumble again as the mighty "Volcan de Fuego" bellowed, it's mighty calls shaking the ground with a force so great that it forced the ground to open and caused boiling steam to gush out to the sky. This volcano was one of several in the area, all the other volcanoes had been dormant for thousands of years. But not this one, the Volcan de Fuego refused to sleep, it gave the villagers a good scare every couple of months. There usually wasn't much to worry about, some grumbling some smoke a few rocks blown into a house or two and then nothing. Nothing for many months in between. But this time things seemed different. The eruptions were louder, the magma was brighter and the lava flowed with ease.

This time the villagers knew that they needed to flee. Nobody wanted to leave, they loved their jungle oasis they were torn, they did not know what to do to escape their fiery fate. Death seemed imminent. Children hugged their mom's out of fear, even the mightiest of warriors had tears in their eyes as they saw their surroundings burn. They all looked to their ancestors for guidance. The elders instructed them to huddled together, and chant. Chant to our ancestors, the group began. After several minutes the chants became louder than the volcano itself. A tremendous bolt of lightning startled the group, they all stopped chanting and looked towards the impact site, there stood a giant Mayan stela-- A large stone with pictographs, appeared that showed them exactly what they needed to do to survive their ordeal. The elders were able to read the stela and interpret its meaning.

The leader of the town rushed to the edge of the river, the stela said we need to gather as many orchid flowers as possible. A special orchid flower named the Monja Blanca or White Nun. The town elders asked all of the young and swift people of the group to run to edge of the river where the Monja Blanca could be found. They placed every flower they could find in baskets and took them to the center of the community where all of the people were gathered. One by one each villager ate a petal, and overwhelming feeling of joy overcame them as they looked at each other and magically turned into Quetzals, a beautiful bird now known as the national bird of a country. As birds the villagers were able to fly free and away from the volcanoes grip. Benjamin's grandpa went on and on about how his ancestors were known as the flying snake people as they had all turned into birds with long tail feathers. "Our people didn't just vanish, it's no mystery to me," he exclaimed in a high pitched, crazy tone of voice with his fist waving in the air.

Everyone in Benjamin's village thought his grandpa was "loco" but not Benjamin, his grandpa's stories always made him smile and think. "What if grandpa wasn't so crazy? What if what he said was true?" He laughed and pretended to fly while he ran through his house and his parents vegetable garden. He flew fast and high and he flew from tree to tree, he flew passed the volcano towards unknown land. Suddenly a loud growl brought him back to reality. A feeling in his gut that he was not able to shake. This was a feeling he had lived with for as long as he could remember. Benjamin or Benny as his family called him, was hungry-again.

There was a smell of burning wood in the air that made his stomach churn and his mouth water. But he knew better. If there was going to be food it would be around noon and only if mom had any leftover tortillas. His mom was a "tortillera"- a lady that made and sold tortillas for a living. Sometimes her customers wouldn't buy all of them so on occasions there was some masa left over for him to fill his belly. Mom would make little tamales with the leftover masa or sometimes she would fill a pitcher of water with sugar and make a sweet masa beverage. In any case, leftover masa was always a good thing.

For now, there was a good amount of a thick drink on the kitchen table that his mom had prepared for him made from oatmeal. "Tomate tu mosh" –Drink your mosh. Benny's mom reminded him.

Benny's family had no refrigerator and they couldn't afford a cow or goats. His house was as clean as you can keep a house with a dirt floor. The roof was made of corrugated metal, the walls were a mix of wood, cardboard, and mud. –Anything his dad could get his hands on that would help keep the rain out.

Benny and his family didn't have much yet they considered themselves lucky. They lived near fertile mountains next to colossal inactive volcanoes lush and full of flowers. His mom and dad were able to grow vegetables, they had chickens and his mom had her tortilla business. They never starved though on many

occasions they did go a little hungry. Somedays they had two meals a day, other days only one and sometimes they had to wait 'til the next day. It all depended on how many tortillas were sold or how many eggs the chickens laid that day or if the bugs and rodents stayed away from the vegetables or how many clients his dad was able to taxi around the pueblo.

Benny's dad was a tuk-tuk driver-Guatemala's version of the Indian rickshaw. These motor cycle taxis were everywhere. Zooming, hundreds of them fighting to transport people from corner to corner. Benny loved it when his dad would offer him a ride before his shift began. Benny's dad would let him stand in the back of taxi while Benny held on with all his strength. The taxi would motor at full speed for a few blocks. Benny would have to walk home as his dad head to work. The Tuk-tuks were usually leased from the company to the person that was driving so Benny's dad did not own the motor bike, and most of the money he made per day would go to the owner of the motor taxi. Benny's family was only allowed to keep about 10 percent of the profits.

Food or no food nothing, money or no money Benny kept smiling. He had a good life, he was kind and smart. Benny was a good kid. He always found ways to help his mom around the house, he always did his homework, always said his prayers, and always listened to his dad. When he wasn't busy with chores, he was swinging in his hammock. His hammock was his comfy bed at night and one of his trusted playmates during the day. If Benny wasn't reading while on his hammock or sleeping in his hammock, then that meant that he was playing games outside with his friends. Soccer with the neighborhood kids while using a small plastic ball was a daily occurrence. All these games and activities helped distract him, especially on the days that he felt those annoying little hunger pains. On many occasions, he would run across his pueblo's lands, running through some of his neighbors' gardens. He would stick his arms out, and pretend to fly. Benjamin would recall his abuelo's stories, his heart would beat rapidly and his imagination would run wild while reciting his grandpa's words. He would close his eyes and instantly turn himself into the majestic little green bird from his grandfather's stories. It was a lovely green bird, its chest full of red feathers. The feathers on its head were shaped in a form of a buzz cut, almost like a flat top. And its tail feathers, those feathers were so long, approximately three to four feet long. Flight for the little green bird was somewhat complicated. But, when it flew, it left everyone in awe. In the sky this little bird was magical. Its wings soared with the wind, tail feathers curling and waving. It was a confusing yet beautiful sight. Anything that got a glimpse of it in the sky would never think it was a bird. It was as if a green snake had grown wings and learned to fly. Many called it just that --the Snake Bird. The bird is named Quetzal, it's the national bird of the country Benjamin and his family are from, the national bird of Guatemala. The Quetzal was happy in its paradise, living a happy humble little green bird life. A yell suddenly startled Quetzal, "Patojos, vengan a comer". Benjamin's mom was calling for him and the rest of the kids to go home to eat lunch.

Benny ran to his house, past his grandfather who was sitting on an old wooden chair made out a semi-precious pink colored wood known as Matilisguate. "Hurry mijo, your mom has been calling you for a while now". "What happened, why did it take you so long to come over"? "Were you daydreaming again", asked grandpa. "I love to fly Abuelo", responded Benjamin. "I wish I could turn into a bird a go anywhere I want."

Noon had come around, the tortilla customers had all left, and yes! There were four unsold tortillas. Crispy, crunchy, and fat, in his culture the tortillas were made thick, they were not the skinny type that other people from other places make tacos with. Benny noticed a pot full of black beans boiling, eggs cooking on the wood stove, chilmol on the molcajete—a Guatemalan tomato sauce made by crushing the ingredients in a stone bowl and mortar, a chicken on the asador (the grille) and a full pitcher of freshly squeezed orange juice. "All this and leftover tortillas", Benny thought to himself. I must be dreaming he said as he salivated and his stomach growled the loudest growl.

That day was special, the family had a guest. A cousin from his mother's side has come from the north. Benjamin had never met him, but he reminded him of a parrot. He would not stop talking. Eventually the conversation bored Benny. Benny started daydreaming while the parrot repeating the same thing over and over. That parrot mentioned a land paved in gold, where the bird nests were huge and soft, the fruit and the veggies were sweeter than sugar cane, and slugs and lizards were plump and juicy. A place, where no bird ever went hungry. A place where if you worked hard, you had a chance to be anything you wanted. Benny's imagination navigated through Cousin parrot's explanations and he went on and on about this wonderful place named America.

Benny's parents were intrigued. And they had some wonderful news to share too. Benny was going to be a big brother. Benny's father shared the news with everyone at the table, they all cheered and hugged his mom. Later that evening Benny caught a conversation between his mother and father. It was obvious that his father could not stop thinking of the wonders that cousin parrot had mentioned.

"What if I left", Benny's father asked his wife. "I could send you, Benny, and the baby lots of money", he told her. But Benny's mother was wise, she knew it was not good to separate the family. The Parrot's conversations also made Benny feel restless. "Could such a wonderful place exist?", he thought to himself.

Months passed; Benny's mother's belly had grown. But things didn't seem to be too good around the house. Mom and dad seemed worried. The tortilla business had too much competition, there were many other people selling tortillas too. His dad's tuk-tuk motor taxi had broken down. It was hard for him to find other jobs. There little bit of savings was dwindling. The family kept thinking about the conversation with their cousin. A decision had to made swiftly.

It was a very difficult moment in their life but Benny's family had finally made up their mind. They would leave as soon as possible. The family sold or gave away everything they had. They were able to get some money for the tortilla comal and for the few items they possessed. Benny's heart was breaking. Grandpa, one of Benny favorite people was too old to make this trip with them so he would stay behind. Benny would have to live the rest of his life without his grandpa.

Benny, grandpa called from his chair, "mijo, remember my stories are true". "The old ways can help you get what you need, the old ways will help you reach your goals"." Never forget where you are from". "Please take this little pouch full of orchid pedals with you where ever you go they will help keep you safe". But Benny ignored grandpa's pleas and left the little pouch on the table.

Chapter 2 All for Nothing

The first signs of the morning came; Benny family started walking towards the main road to catch a local chicken bus headed towards the border. From the corner of his eye Benny sees his good friend, a kid nicknamed Gallito (Little Rooster), Gallito was loud and never combed his brown/reddish hair. He reminded everyone in town of a Rooster especially when he came to visit in the morning. Gallito looked up and saw Benny waving goodbye. "I'm leaving to find a better place to live", said Benny. "Better than this?" "But this place is wonderful", thought Gallito to himself. Gallito waved back at Benny and wished him well. The family got on a bus and left for the Mexican-Guatemalan border. Guatemalans are allowed to cross the Mexican border and travel to Mexico City without a special Visa, but that's it, they can't legally go any further north. The trip took several days, it was hot and crowded. Once the family got to the city, it was time to walk north. Until they reached a group of migrants that had walked all the way from Colombia, South America.

Quetzal and his family flew for a very long time. The bird's wings were so tired; its stomach was growling. "If I wasn't so hungry, this place we're flying through would be very pleasant", he murmured. The landscape was green and lush, it had not changed much from his lands. Quetzal noticed that it was getting dark. The moon was up just above the mountains. "The moon looks so huge", the little green bird quietly whispered to itself. The Quetzal heard his mother—Benny a dormir. Benny's mother laid next him as they camped under the stars. She covered him with a thick blue blanket.

Quetzal found the nearest tree, it also found a few lizards to munch on. With a full belly, the little green bird slept well for the night. The next morning Quetzal was on its way again but this time only for a short time before it started noticing the landscape. It had changed. Quetzal noticed the sun beating down on its neck, it was hot. Quetzal felt drained and thirsty, the little green bird needed water. Quetzal saw a small pond. "What a sight for sore eyes", it screeched –as it dove down to it. The little green bird drank until its heart's content. While Quetzal focused on the water it also looked around at its surroundings. The land was full of thorny cacti and small shrubbery. It was barren and dry. Quetzal had entered Golden Eagle territory. The little green bird had heard stories of Golden Eagles, they were strong, ruthless, and extremely territorial. They didn't take too kindly to strangers. But the little green bird was too thirsty to think about eagles or any other thing plus it too was a confident bird, it was also brave and mighty. A Quetzal could fend for itself.

The little green bird's long tail feathers moved and twisted with every gulp of water, that movement caught the attention of a stranger. An eagle's call was heard in the background. Quetzal wasn't sure what to make of the sound, but something told him that he needed to be ready for anything. The little green bird still hadn't been able to quench its thirst so it kept drinking. "Golden Eagles are expert hunters", Quetzal recalled while he gulped water. The little green bird was correct. Golden Eagles were fierce and admired by all the other animals in the desert lands. Their long claws are sharp and ready to strike at anything that crosses their path. They specialize in hunting snakes. Unbeknownst to Quetzal, a Golden Eagle stood at a top of a giant cactus only a few feet where it was drinking water. "Strange for a snake to expose itself like that", thought Golden Eagle. "It's about 3 feet long, plump and green, it's going to make for a good meal," Golden Eagle, thought as it salivated.

Golden Eagle dove down-- claws first. Quetzal saw a shadow and flew backward causing Eagle to miss and grab a claw full of dirt. "What, you have wings? "What are you", asked Eagle. "A bird, a snake, or both? I've never seen anything like you".

"I am Quetzal", yelled the little green bird. While striking Golden Eagle's right eye with the tip of his sharp tail feathers. "Next time, I'll strike you with my beak", said Quetzal. "What are you doing, drinking my water and eating my lizards?" Golden Eagle demanded an answer. "You don't belong here", it continued. "You must go, go back to where you came from". Quetzal and Golden Eagles spoke the same language. They just sounded a little different. But they could understand each other perfectly. "I am not here to stay", said Quetzal, "I am only passing by". But Golden Eagle ignored Quetzal and called to its flock. "See this little green thing?" "It is here to steal our food and water". "It threatened to leave me blind by pecking my eyes out". Golden Eagle convinced his flock that Quetzal was bad so they all screeched and yelled, get out, get out!

They dove and clawed at the little green bird, they chased it relentlessly. "Stay on your side". "You don't belong here", they yelled. The bus ride was long and the miles of walking were so tiring but Benny understood why they had turned around and were heading back home. He understood why they were getting a bus back to their country. His father had a black eye, and even his mother had several bruises on her arms and legs as she was pushed by an angry, hostile individual. "Vayanse de aqui, no los queremos an nuestras tierras"—they repeated. Little Benny felt so much pain so much sadness.

Chapter 3 Must-Try Again

One of Quetzal's wings had been scratched down to the bone, and the little bird had been bruised

and almost beaten to death. It took Quetzal weeks to heal and even longer to grow most of its feathers

back. But even in such pain, all Quetzal could do was think about the conversation his dad had with

cousin parrot. Parrot's stories of such wonderful lands were stuck in his head. The thought of a better

place to live was clinging to his heart. Quetzal wanted to visit, it wanted to live in such a wonderful

place.

Not knowing what to do, Quetzal looked for his grandfather for advice.

"Grand Son", he said, "I too have heard of wonderful lands but then I look around and I see

wonderful lands here". "Here, I see happiness, here I see plenty of everything". 'Look around you"?

But Quetzal was a stubborn little green bird. It could no longer appreciate the wonders that surrounded

it. He only saw the negative. I don't want to be hungry. I want to be able to buy things whenever I

want. Quetzal only saw what Parrot had put in its imagination. The little green bird couldn't help but

think about how ugly and poor everything looked around it especially compared to the wonders Parrot

had described.

Abuelo knew that there was no convincing Quetzal to stay and appreciate what he had. "Son, I

see in your eyes that no matter what I say, you are willing to risk everything for this new life".

"If you must go you will need luck and most importantly some divine intervention". "I wish you well, and hope that we see each other again someday", said Grandfather as tears rolled down his cheeks. "Before you travel, make sure you pick a full-bloomed white nun, our land's flower, it's a special orchid". "Like the ones I tried giving you and your family tried making this trip the first time". "Remember you can find those flowers deep in the forest". "Si abuelo", Benny nodded, "I'll use them this time". "When a pedal is eaten, combined with a fruit or flower of another land, the combination will turn you into something very special", explained grandfather. "Take my advice and you will reach your destination". "Le prometo que le voy hacer caso", "I promise I will do it", Benny reiterated.

Benny's father had heard that several groups of people were migrating to the United States this time from Honduras, they had walked for weeks. They were planning to pass by Benny's town in Guatemala and Benny's dad was going to join them. The plan this time was for Benny's dad to head out, Benny's mom was too many month along in her pregnancy to risk the trip. Benny knew he couldn't let his dad go alone.

Chapter 4 Blind Eye

Weeks passed until Quetzal felt well enough to try his journey once more. This time it would be different, this time he had learned from his mistakes and this time he would follow his Grandfather's special orchid advise. Quetzal again flew for a very long distance until it reached Golden Eagle territory, it flew low and stealthy. It passed the spot where the flock had beat him until they run him out. It looked up at the blue sky searching for adversaries but it only saw a couple of monarch butterflies flying around. Quetzal scanned the landscape, it got lucky, no one seemed to be around for the moment.

"This is as far as my family went last time", it thought to itself. Quetzal knew in his heart that it wouldn't be able to travel any further as long as those snake-hunting Golden Eagles were around. "Is this where I'm supposed to eat my Grandfather's flower recipe?" "It must be, I see no other way", thought Quetzal.

Quetzal wondered what to eat from this vastly arid land. There didn't seem to be any appetizing fruits or flowers. Though there were several lizards and snakes, his Abuelo said he needed to combine its flower's pedal with a flower or fruit from the local area. Then Quetzal remembered that when it first saw a Golden Eagle, it was perched on a cactus. That cactus had a red pear-like fruit sticking out of it. Quetzal flew to the top of the nearest cactus. There was a large reddish fruit hanging there but it was full of thorns. The little green bird desperately picked a thorn off, one at a time. Quetzal had never seen this fruit in its land. "I wonder what it tastes like", it thought. Quetzal felt like it had been removing thorns for hours, then suddenly, off in the distance it heard the eagles call. "Leave our Tunas alone", cried the voices off in the distance. Quetzal hurried to eat the red fruit, "I guess these things are called Tunas" it thought, as it swallowed pieces of the fruit along with a few thorns. "Mmmm", it barely had time to contemplate the sweet taste of the Prickly Pear. In its panic, the little green bird almost forgot the pedal from the white orchid.

Quetzal managed to get the pedal from under his right-wing and eat it, as it scurried down the cactus. Quetzal's stomach started grumbling. Its forehead was sweating and its feathers started to burn. The flock of Golden Eagles swept down mightily, claws first. There was a dreadful scuffle. Thick dust clouds formed. Dirt, feathers, and blood were flung everywhere. When it was all done, there was no little green bird left.

There were so many feathers on the ground—too many to count. The Golden Eagles, in their anger and frenzy, lost track of the little green bird. Then the flock noticed that their leader was being held by its neck, a powerful claw tightening its grip". "What are you doing?", questioned one of the Eagles.

"Just passing by said the powerful bird. "Dejalo ir, let him go, Roadrunner, we have no problemas with you". "Roadrunner"? Quetzal thought to itself, "was this the special power of the orchid?" "It must be," Quetzal laughed inside, but did not share its joy out loud. It squeezed a little harder, Quetzal could tell that the Golden Eagle, it had in its grasp, was the one that had hurt him and his family months ago. Quetzal knew this because this eagle's eye was still infected from the puncture wound of their previous scuffle. Quetzal laughed again, this time out loud. It threw the partly blind eagle to the side and ran off into the sunset, leaving a trail of dust in its path.

Chapter 5 Miles and Miles Sin Comer

Being a Roadrunner had its advantages. Roadrunner (Quetzal) was now brownish grey, except for one red and one green feather he had under his right-wing. For the most part, it blended in with its surroundings. Roadrunner (Quetzal) also spoke the language, turns out roadrunner and quetzal are very similar languages. "As a quetzal, I ate lizards, those aren't bad, but snakes, now that's good eating", it thought. Roadrunner (Quetzal) did feel a little frustrated because it could only fly or glide for very short distances. But the lack of flight was made up by its super running ability, it was extremely fast on land and no longer had to worry about the Golden Eagles, they didn't even pay attention to him now. He blended in perfectly.

Roadrunner (Quetzal) headed for its paradise. It walked and ran for weeks. During his travel Benny found the courage to tell his father that he too had joined the caravan for America. Benny's father cried but was very happy to see him. Mijo, son he said while tears rolled down his face. Benny kept waiting for a angry lecture but there was nothing, just a sigh and a big huge.

Benny and his dad walked together for several weeks. Stopping to drink water and occasionally stopping to eat. But most of the time there was no food around. The hunger pains were unbearable, but Benny kept going, he knew that with every step it took, it was closer to its dream. Benny's feet hurt, he was tired he needed a faster way to get where he was going. One terrible night, while the group was trying to hide from the local Mexican police. The abandoned shack they had chosen was full of insects and a snake. The place also belonged to the local cartel, they claimed that because the group used their property they now had to pay them rent. During the confusion Benny lost track of his father, he searched and search but he was nowhere to be found. The group ran to get away from a drug cartel that tried to extort them.

Benny was so tired, so hungry and so scared. During his travels, many people had mentioned something about a train. "El Tren de la Muerte", the train of death, he thought "I don't know about that, but according to many people it will save me several weeks of walking.

He made up his mind, he could climb the train. He headed towards the nearest train station. But neither he nor the people from the caravan were welcome there, so they could not purchase tickets, if they wanted a train ride, they would have to climb the top of the train and ride it, in that manner. It was days of riding the train. Cold nights of holding on to whatever he could so that he would not fall off. Some days people would climb the train and sell water or food on other days people with guns would climb the train and charge a riding fee, Benny would always find a place to hide. After eight days of riding the train, Benny could not take it anymore he decided to jump off. But the decision of getting off the train meant he had to walk for many miles.

One particular night Benny felt so hungry that he could not fall asleep. It was very late, Roadrunner (Quetzal) kept hearing several strange noises. It was his stomach, the bird was super hungry. "This has happened too often in my life", thought the little green bird as its stomach roared. It had been three days since his last snake. And now it was too dark, it was too cold for them to slither around. Roadrunner (Quetzal) noticed movement in the night sky and a sort of clicking sound. "Maybe it's something I could eat", but there was nothing. Benny was dizzy from the pain, he missed his family, but he kept moving forward. The trek through the dessert had been brutal. He came across a very humble little house, that somewhat reminded him of his. He cried as he got to the front door and collapsed. Benny wasn't sure if he was delirious or if he was dreaming but out of the beautiful little house out came a giant hummingbird. The hummingbird made Benny feel safe, she fed him for a few days and she encouraged him to finish his journey.

At last Benjamin found his destination, or so he thought. As Roadrunner looked into the distance it noticed a great wall. "How am I supposed to get over this", it pondered. Roadrunner (Quetzal) knew his Road Running days were coming to an end. Its running skills had gotten it as far as they could. The little green bird spent several days looking at the large obstacle pondering its next move.

Chapter 6 Crossing

The sky was dark again, this time there were no stars, and the moon was hiding. Off in the distance, a storm raged with thunder. Suddenly, a shadow spoke to him, "Hey roadrunners aren't' supposed to have any red or green feathers". "Yeah, I noticed your right-wing, you aren't from here, are you"? said the shadowy figure.

"I'm just passing by", said Roadrunner (Quetzal). As the dark figure got closer. Suddenly it let out a great howl. That noise made Roadrunner's (Quetzal) blood boil, something inside immediately prepared him for a fight. Roadrunner (Quetzal) knew what that figure was, —a Coyote. Roadrunner's (Quetzal) feathers ruffled its leg muscles got tight. "Relax", said the Coyote to the Roadrunner (Quetzal). "I don't want to fight with anybody". I just came to offer some help. I'm an expert at going around this wall and getting people to the other side.

Coyote went on and asked if Roadrunner (Quetzal) knew how to get around the wall. "I'm assuming the reason you are here pacing back and forth is that you want to cross". "I can take you around this wall to a river crossing if you'd like". "I know this area like the back of my paw". "I only ask that after I get you across you pay me". Roadrunner (Quetzal) was silent, he wanted to cross. It knew a wonderful land and great opportunities waited on the other side; its dreams would finally come true. But what of Coyote's payment, what would it want, how much would it want? Roadrunner (Quetzal) had nothing to offer.

Later that night Roadrunner (Quetzal) heard screeching and chicken-like noises. There was also a lot of peaking and scurrying around. It was other Roadrunners and they all headed in the same direction, all running and hiding from something. Some Roadrunners were chasing snakes for a quick meal. Some, it seemed, were being helped by Coyotes. Others seemed to be lost aimlessly wandering the desert. Roadrunner (Quetzal) didn't trust Coyote so it didn't take its offer. Instead, Roadrunner (Quetzal) followed a flock of Roadrunners, eventually, they reached a river, it was a grand river. It's water cold, turbulent, and fast. The river was wide and deep. Roadrunner (Quetzal), could not fly for long distances and so it couldn't fly across.

As a Roadrunner he was going to have to do something it has never had to do as before as a Quetzal, it was going to have to swim. "Get in the water, stay low", it said to itself as it shivered. The water was cold and it had a strange taste. "What am I doing"? "Why am I here, at home, I was a symbol of liberty and a sign of freedom." "Now, I'm cold and my legs, my arms, my chest, my back are all wet," thought the little green bird to itself as tears mixed with the water of the river.

Soaking wet, shivering, tired, and hungry, Roadrunner (Quetzal) got to the side of the river. Roadrunner (Quetzal) noticed a strange smell. The air smelled like a wet dog. It was that Coyote. Coyote's mouth was full. It had another roadrunner by the neck. "What are you doing?", yelled Roadrunner (Quetzal). "Payment", mumbled back Coyote as it swallowed a morsel of the bird it had in its mouth and lunged after Roadrunner (Quetzal) "I don't owe you anything", yelled Roadrunner (Quetzal). I got myself across, yelled Benny as he ran as fast as its Roadrunner feet could take it.

Chapter 7 Illusions

The chase between these two lasted for days. One day after running and running for hours, Roadrunner (Quetzal) found a field full of corn. It was hungry and delighted in the sweet corn. It ate until its stomach ached. Roadrunner (Quetzal) was so busy eating that it did not notice Coyote had finally caught up to him. Coyote jumped to grasp its next meal. But Quetzal was not an ordinary Roadrunner. He fought back. There was a dreadful scuffle. Roadrunner (Quetzal) had to think fast, what would happen if it ate some corn and a pedal from the orchid, which it carried tucked under its right-wing. Thick dust clouds formed. There was a dreadful scuffle. Thick dust clouds formed. Dirt, feathers, and blood were flung everywhere. When it was all done, there was no Roadrunner left.

 Out of the chaos, a black crow appeared. It flapped its wings and sure enough, under its right-wing, it had green and red feathers. It's tail feathers were brown instead of black. It was Quetzal-now a crow, it felt strong and smart but best of all it was able to fly again. Crow (Quetzal) took to the sky. Coyote was left with an injured eye wondering where the devious roadrunner had gone.

As a crow, Quetzal was able to fly long distances. It eventually met other crows. They were so friendly. The entire group would try to communicate with Quetzal at once, but Quetzal could not understand. Their language was not familiar. Quetzals, Roadrunners, and even Coyotes spoke the same language. But Crows, they were different.

Crow (Quetzal) could see that all the crows he knew lived together in an enormous tree. The tree was their roost site, their home. Hundreds of crows welcomed Crow (Quetzal). It made several friends despite its difference in appearance. They all noticed the extra green and red feathers it had underneath its right-wing and the brown tail feathers. Crow (Quetzal) mostly communicated with them using signs and pointing at things. The other crows thought that Crow (Quetzal) must have fallen off the nest when it was a baby. They

thought it was a slow crow. Eventually, after many months of congregating with them, Crow (Quetzal) started understanding their stories. Benny started understanding their language.

The flock of crows was happy. They loved collecting shiny little items. Every nest was decorated with what they considered beautiful jewelry. Every night Crow (Quetzal) and his friends would fly down to the farms to eat as much corn and worms as they could and collect anything shiny that was accidentally dropped by the farmers.

One morning while Crow (Quetzal) and his friends were making fun of the pigs wallowing in the mud. Crow (Quetzal) noticed a white bird. "What's that, do crows come in different colors? Crow (Quetzal) asked his friends. "No", they explained. "That's a Seagull, they live on the other side of town by the beach". Don't know what it's doing here though, but that's enough of that they all agreed. The crows decided to chase the seagull out of their farmland. Crow (Quetzal) joined the flock at first, chasing the Seagull out of the farm every day. Making fun of it for smelling like fish and having white feathers instead of black ones.

But it never really felt right to make fun of the Seagull especially because Crow (Quetzal) didn't exactly have all black feathers either. One-day Crow (Quetzal) remembered what the Golden Eagles had done to him so many months ago. Crow (Quetzal) decided not to chase the Seagull out of the farm anymore. Instead, Crow (Quetzal) had made up its mind that it would become that Seagull's friend.

Crow (Quetzal) would meet the Seagull during the early morning before the other crow noticed. Quetzal would bring a mouth full of corn and worms. "For you", it would say, not sure if the Seagull would understand its language. Turns out that

Crows and Seagulls understood each other perfectly. Seagull was grateful it hadn't been able to catch food for itself after the accident. Seagull mentioned to Crow (Quetzal) that it was lost and would get very dizzy. "that's why I don't leave very far after your friends chase me away. I don't know where to go". "Life by the sea is so much better than this", Seagull would say. "But I don't remember how to get there".

For several weeks Seagull and Crow (Quetzal) would meet and talk about the sea. It sounded wonderful to Crow (Quetzal) and though there was nothing wrong with living as a Crow, it was not exactly the life it had imagined. It was not what he wanted. Crow (Quetzal) became determined to help Seagull find its home. Crow(Quetzal) remembered that many rivers went through his town, he remembered abuelo that all rivers lead to the ocean. Crow (Quetzal) mentioned this to his friend so two nights later they decided to follow the river downstream. They followed the river for hours, winding through the mountains up and down the valleys until it started to smell strange. It smelled different. There was a smell of salt in the air. What's that smell?" asked Crow (Quetzal). "It's the Ocean!" Seagull replied. What's that sound? Asked Crow (Quetzal). It's the waves crashing, replied Seagull. The birds flew faster and faster to reach their destination. Quetzal could feel the ocean breeze through its feathers. It was wonderful.

After a few hours of splashing about in the water Crow (Quetzal) noticed that his friend the Seagull had stopped splashing back and was now focused on something else. Crow (Quetzal) too stopped splashing as it noticed that they had been surrounded by hundreds of seabirds. Pelican, Tern, Albatross, Booby, and Seagulls, hundreds of them surrounded the two friends. "Crows, should stay on their side, why are you here?" asked the mob. "Just passing by", said Crow (Quetzal).

"No", yelled a big strange-looking bird, its peak was so big and bag-like it could probably fit tons of food into it. "It's not natural for a Crow and a Seagull to be friends". The pelican explained. "You must go back to wherever you came from". Seagull tried to intervene explaining that Crow(Quetzal) had helped it. "Don't you see if it wasn't for my friend, I wouldn't have been able to get back home", Seagull explained. But no one listened. Seagull pleaded but it seemed like all of the birds of the sea were against their friendship. They all started screeching and yelling, Leave, leave, leave. Even as the two friends tried to comply, the mob got louder and blocked their way out. Hundreds of birds chased Crow(Quetzal) and Seagull, hurting them in the process.

Chapter 8 Not for me

In the scuffle, Crow (Quetzal) lost sight of his Seagull friend and was pushed by a flock of pelicans into the rotting wooden pillars of an old pier. The Crow's wing was injured again. Its wing had never quite recovered from the beating it had received from the Golden Eagles. With all the commotion, the barking of seals, waves crashing, hundreds of birds screeching—noises everywhere, Crow (Quetzal) panicked. Crow(Quetzal) cried for the first time since it decided to come to this great place. "All its effort, all the pain and suffering it had endured, just to die, here by this rotten pile of junk," thought Crow (Quetzal) was scared; it didn't know what to do.

The sea birds kept pushing and pecking at Crow (Quetzal). They threw and kicked sand at its eyes. They were relentless in their assault. The mob pushed until Crow (Quetzal) was neck-deep into the water. Soaking wet and cold, the waves crashing on its back; the poor little bird was drowning. Crow (Quetzal) desperately looked around for anything it could grab on to. It noticed a bunch of green leaves floating. Quetzal grabbed them but they did not hold him afloat. The more it struggled to stay afloat the more the leaves tangled around its body. Desperate to save its life Crow (Quetzal) remembered its Grandfather's recipe. Crow(Quetzal) reached for one of its last Orchid pedals which he kept tucked away underneath his red feather. He quickly ate it along with the only flower/fruit-looking thing around—the green floating leaves. No sooner had Crow (Quetzal) eaten his grandfather's mix than hundreds of sea birds jumped on it making sure Crow's (Quetzal's) beak was underwater. There was a dreadful scuffle. Thick salty mist clouds formed. Ocean water, feathers, and blood were flung everywhere. When it was all done, there was no Crow left. Suddenly, out of the water flew a stealthy fast-flying Seagull. "Where did that good for nothing Crow go?" asked the angry seabirds. "Hopefully its underwater." "It didn't belong here," mumbled one of the bigger birds.

Crow (Quetzal) now a Seagull, flew frantically to the last place it remembered seeing its Seagull friend. Seagull (Quetzal) found it bruised and hiding under a bench made of concrete. "Leave me alone," cried Seagull's (Quetzal's) friend thought it was another sea bird looking to hurt it some more. "It's me" cried, Seagull (Quetzal). I'm so sorry this happened to you". The Seagull recognized the voice and the red and green feather hanging from inside its right wing and the brown tail feathers "Crow?" asked Seagull's (Quetzal's) friend.

The two Seagull friends lived together for a long time. Life by the sea was nice. The breeze was always wonderful. There was plenty of fish to eat. But the fish always tasted strange, they were almost always covered in tar. Both Seagull (Quetzal) and its friend had lots of fun together, though all the other seagulls always thought there was something strange about Seagull (Quetzal). They didn't like the crazy-colored feathers under its right-wing. Brown tail feathers and black crest feathers. It just wasn't what others were used to.

One morning the seagull flock was in a frenzy. What's going on? asked Quetzal. We're all going

to get something different to eat. They flocked and headed over to the nearest school cafeteria. While

eating leftover lunches from the school trash bin Seagull (Quetzal) realized that this was not the

paradise he had imagined. The trips to the school trash bin

were frequent. There was always leftover pizza or peanut butter

bread or coffee cake, chalupas, or hamburgers. The stuff was tasty

but Seagull (Quetzal) knew in his heart that this was not the paradise

he wanted.

"None of this food is fresh, why am I eating from a trash bin?"

While chewing on a leftover chimichanga Seagull (Quetzal) noticed

several shadows lurking under the trash bin. It was dozens of rats,

looking for a meal too.

This is our territory said the rats. You need to leave. Before Seagull (Quetzal) could say a word, they had jumped all over him. They chewed on his wings, Quetzal could no longer fly, he ran as fast as he could away from the trash. He was able to get away from most of the rats but two were still gnawing at his legs. Help he cried, but no one came to help him. In a last-ditch effort to save his life he reached for his last crumbled-up flower piece of pedal, he grabbed the closest flower to the him, a red rose. Dust clouds formed--dirt was everywhere. The rats were left th a hand full of white feathers. "Where did that Seagull go"? they asked. Seconds before they were swallowed whole by a Giant Bald Eagle.

Seagull (Quetzal) had turned into a confident, strong Bald Eagle. Flying free in a land of plenty. He flew as high as he could over the mountain tops. He noticed a flock of Bald Eagles calling to him. He joined them and flew with them for a few weeks.

Most of the time Bald Eagle (Quetzal) tried hiding his colored feathers. "Bald Eagles aren't supposed to have so many different colored feathers", he thought to himself and "when I speak, I sound a little different from the others". He wondered why none of the other Bald Eagles had ever said anything about his different colored feathers. But they did notice, it just didn't matter. It's okay to be different. He finally had a conversation with one of them and it asked. "Are you not from here?" "I'm just passing by", Bald Eagle (Quetzal) quickly responded his typical answer. But this time that was a lie. Bald Eagle (Quetzal) had arrived at this destination. It was here to stay. After much suffering, after all the hunger, loneliness, cold, and pain. It had reached its goal.

Bald Eagle (Quetzal) had a happy life; it never went hungry. As an American Bald Eagle, Quetzal was now one of the most powerful birds in the world. It was able to fly where ever it wanted, Bald Eagle (Quetzal) had free range of the land as far as it could see. It turns out that having different colored feathers didn't matter, all bald eagles were unique.

And yet as the years passed there always seemed to be something missing. Benny wasn't sure what it was. Maybe he missed his home or he missed his family whatever it was, there was an unexplainable feeling. There was always a void.

Cousin Parrot was correct; this place is beautiful. It's like nothing else on Earth. But both Cousin Parrot and Grandfather forgot to tell Quetzal that all of its experiences and the time spent living as a different bird, would have a great impact on him. Quetzal would never be seen as a native bird in its homeland ever again. And he would always be a little different from the other Bald Eagles.

Quetzal had turned into a strong American Bald Eagle, with the running skills of a Roadrunner, the cunning of a Crow, the stealth of a Seagull, and the heart and soul of a brave little green bird.

THE END

Good night, to my half Quetzal/half Golden Eagle yet all American Bald Eagle Kiddos, I love you both with all my heart. Que Dios me los cuide y los bendiga siempre.

Love Dad.

Made in the USA
Las Vegas, NV
14 February 2024

85764138R00026